BMX
BRAVERY

BY JAKE MADDOX

text by
Brandon Terrell

STONE ARCH BOOKS
a capstone imprint

Jake Maddox JV books are published by Stone Arch Books
A Capstone Imprint
1710 Roe Crest Drive
North Mankato, Minnesota 56003
www.mycapstone.com

Library of Congress Cataloging-in-Publication Data

Maddox, Jake, author.
BMX bravery / [text] by Brandon Terrell.
    pages cm. -- (Jake Maddox. Jake Maddox JV)
 Summary: Fourteen-year-old Cam loves riding BMX bikes, but he is also a careful rider—
but when his new friend insists on trying out a particularly dangerous course and breaks
his leg on a jump, Cam has to ride the Copper Devil trail alone in order to get help.

ISBN 978-1-4965-2630-4 (library binding)
ISBN 978-1-4965-2632-8 (pbk.)
 ISBN 978-1-4965-2634-2 (ebook pdf)

1. Bicycle motocross—Juvenile fiction. 2. BMX bikes--Juvenile fiction. 3. Courage--Juvenile
fiction. 4. Self-confidence—Juvenile fiction. 5. Friendship—Juvenile fiction. [1. Bicycle
motocross—Fiction. 2. Courage—Fiction. 3. Self-confidence—Fiction. 4. Friendship—
Fiction.] I. Terrell, Brandon, 1978- author. II. Title.

 PZ7.M25643Bl 2016

 813.6—dc23

 [Fic]

                                    2015035784

Editor: Nate LeBoutillier
Art Director: Russell Griesmer
Designer: Kyle Grenz
Production Specialist: Laura Manthe

Photo Credits:
Shuttterstock

Printed in the United States of America in Stevens Point, Wisconsin.
092015   009222WZS16

TABLE OF CONTENTS

CHAPTER 1

SOLO

Cam Dexter pedaled fast, hit the dirt jump hard, and soared into the air. It was an amazing feeling, cutting through the blue sky, wind against his face, completely airborne. Like flying. But he was also aware of the ground, of the inevitable landing. He gently tapped his bike's brake at the perfect time. This made his front wheel point down, setting him up for a perfect landing. He braced himself, bent his knees, and hit the packed earth of the landing ramp right where he wanted to hit it, right where he always hit it.

Nothin' fancy, no mistakes, he thought as he sped down the dirt ramp.

Cam had been racing the BMX dirt tracks out at Copper Ridge Park since the day his training wheels had come off and he'd wobbled back and forth on his first bike. He loved that bike, still had it hanging in his parents' garage at home. It was powder blue, and he used to tuck baseball cards in the spokes so they clacked and rattled and sounded like a motor as he biked down the road. He'd raced this particular practice course hundreds of times, knew every curve, every berm, every double jump.

Cam shifted his weight to his right side to counter the course's final turn. His bike swung left around the curve, and he applied the brakes again. His speed was cut nearly in half as he rolled safely across the finish line.

"Hey!" a voice called out from behind him. "Why'd you slow down at the end?"

Cam peeled off his helmet and goggles and wiped his sweaty forehead with one arm. He could feel the smear of dirt left behind by his action. Perched on their bikes nearby were two boys and a girl. They all looked to be about fourteen, Cam's age. He didn't recognize them.

Must be out-of-towners, he thought.

The boy in front had a shock of blonde hair. "Why'd you hit the brakes?" he repeated.

"Are you crazy?" Cam asked. "If I hadn't slowed down, I'd have crashed."

The boy shrugged. "Or you'd have beaten your time by over a second. In a race, that's the difference between first and last place, man."

"Thanks for the tip." Cam didn't need any coaching advice. He'd raced for years now, traveling all over Utah and the surrounding states.

"You wanna race?" the girl asked. She had a bright yellow helmet with twin licorice whip pigtails sticking out of either side.

Cam looked around at the dirt track. It was a sunny day, and the place was packed. Kids rode their bikes on different tracks or performed a variety of moves on the nearby street course. Others sat at picnic benches talking and laughing and eating food from a concession stand. Cam was riding alone, like always. He had a couple of buddies from school who liked to hang out and play video games and stuff, but none of them were into BMX.

The blonde kid jutted out his chin. "Name's Jack," he said.

"Cam."

"I'm Ayla," the girl said. She nodded at the quiet boy, who was bunny hopping his bike and not paying much attention to them. "That's Peter."

"Well," Jack said. "Whaddaya say, dude? Wanna race?"

Cam shrugged. "Sure. Why not?"

"Cool." Ayla smiled at him as the quartet spun

their bikes around. Cam followed as they headed toward Ridge Rider, the park's supercross track. Ridge Rider was way more challenging than any other tracks. The jumps were huge, and the few times Cam had tried it, he'd fallen hard on the massive triple jump at the end. No way he wanted to race Ridge Rider.

"Let's race Boulder Pass," Cam suggested, pointing to the practice course he'd just finished.

"Nah," said Jack. "Ridge Rider's more fun."

"I don't know . . . . " Cam said, trailing off. He wanted to back out but didn't want to look like a wuss in front of the other bikers.

"Don't know about what?" Ayla asked. All three kids looked at him.

Cam shook his head. "Never mind."

As they rode across the park, toward the starting ramp of Ridge Rider, Cam tried his hardest to smile, act cool, and not flip his bike around to ditch the trio of teens.

The start of Ridge Rider had a steep scaffold start ramp. The four kids lined up side by side. Cam was on the end, next to Jack. His blonde hair was now hidden under an unscuffed silver helmet. He also had a new, lightweight Redline bike. Cam wrung his well-worn grips. His bike used to be his dad's when he was younger. Cam had fixed it up, using a chunk of his lawn mowing money to buy new twenty-inch tires at the end of last summer.

"Ready?" Jack asked.

Cam tugged his helmet. "Ready as I'll ever be."

"Go!"

The four teens took off down the start ramp. Cam easily kept pace. When they hit the course's first of four tight turns, Cam surprised himself and maneuvered through it smoothly. Peter didn't fare as well. He found himself too far up the track, hitting the top of the curve, overcompensating, and flipping his bike. He bailed, landing safely in the dirt while his bike tumbled end over end.

Cam was clear and focused. They rode furiously through a series of small berms, followed by a step-up. His bike bucked and rocked under him, but he kept control. Around another curve and into a technical "rhythm" section of hills. Through the third turn. Then the fourth. Jack kept pace with him, and Ayla looked smooth and confident over the hills. She leaned forward on her bike. Unless Cam was mistaken, she was smiling.

Coming into the home stretch, the riders were neck and neck. They shot up the first hill and caught air at the same time.

"Woo hoo!" Jack shouted.

Cam was too frightened to be carefree. He looked for the landing and pumped his brake like he always did. His bike tilted down, but he could see he was not going to make it. Not by a long shot.

"Oh no!" he shouted as his front tire hit the lip of the third jump and sent him sailing off his bike.

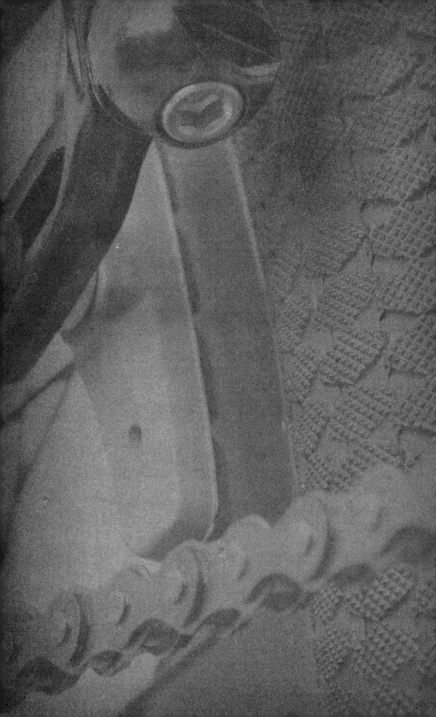

CHAPTER 2

WOUNDED EGO

Cam toppled to the dirt. It wasn't the first time he'd been thrown off his bike. He knew how to tuck and roll. But when he hit the ground, his padded elbow struck the hard-packed earth and pain shot up his arm to his shoulder.

"Ahh!" he cried as Jack and Ayla easily cleared the jump, leaving Cam in the dust.

Cam staggered to his feet, shaking his injured arm. Sure it stung, but his pride was hurt more. He retrieved his bike and walked it to the finish line.

Jack and Ayla were waiting for him.

"That course, man . . . . " Jack flipped his goggles onto his helmet. "That ain't for beginners."

"I almost had to bail after that last jump," Ayla said. She nodded at Cam. "You okay?"

Cam nodded. "Yeah," he grumbled. "Fine."

"Heads up!" Jack shouted, pointing behind Cam. Cam turned just in time to see Peter sail over the final jump, his handlebars turned backward and his arms crossed in a move called an X-up. He landed the X-up perfectly, and skidded to a stop near the others.

"That was sick!" Ayla said, bumping fists with Peter.

Peter simply smiled.

Cam was angry and frustrated and deeply disappointed. He was a safe rider, smart, alert. He never took chances, and yet he looked like a noob in front of these kids because he couldn't land a stupid triple jump.

"How 'bout we give it another run?" Cam offered.

"Nah, man," Jack said. "We've gotta jet."

"Nice ridin' with you," Ayla added.

Jack offered his fist, and Cam begrudgingly bumped it. Ayla and Peter did the same. They rode off together, laughing and joking.

Discouraged, Cam rode out of the park, back toward home.

Alone.

Again.

***

The town of Copper Ridge was nestled right at the base of the Rocky Mountains. Even though Cam had lived there all his life, seeing the jagged peaks towering to the west never failed to take his breath away. The town was small — its main street had just a single stoplight — but it was always bustling with activity and life. Travelers came from all over for the mountainous biking and hiking

trails and to fly fish and camp along the riverbanks nearby.

Cam lived in the middle of town. He buzzed down the main strip, still decked out in pads and helmet. Gift shops and sporting goods stores and restaurants whizzed by on both sides. He caught a whiff of pizza as he buzzed past Benny's, his favorite place to eat. It reminded him that he hadn't really had anything since breakfast, about eight hours ago. His stomach begged him to stop for a slice, but he kept riding home.

Straight ahead, hung across Main Street between two streetlights, was an enormous blue banner. It read: *FIRST ANNUAL COPPER RIDGE BMX RACES!! SIGN UP NOW!! ALL AGE GROUPS!!*

Only two months away! Cam thought with a mixture of excitement and nervousness. He was already signed up in his age bracket. The races were being held at Copper Ridge, most likely on

Ridge Rider. Just the thought of maneuvering the course again brought a fresh throb of pain to Cam's arm.

Cam's street was lined with tall ash trees and houses that all looked like one another. As he bunny-hopped off the curb, Cam noticed a moving truck parked on his block. It was bright white, with the company name in red cursive along the side. The truck was parked in front of the old Hoffstead house. Mr. and Mrs. Hoffstead had sold it a couple of months ago and moved out, but no one had moved in.

Until today, Cam thought.

As he coasted toward his driveway, Cam took both hands off the grips and pulled off his helmet and goggles. He kept his eyes on the moving truck, looking for any sign of his new neighbors.

Cam curved into the long, cracked driveway in front of his house, slowed with a tap of the brakes, and rolled right up to the detached garage. There,

he leaned his bike against the siding, bounded up the cement steps leading to the house's side door, and unlocked it.

"Hello?" he called as he stepped into the quiet house. "Mom? Are you home?"

She didn't answer, which was no surprise. His mom worked long hours at Kingston Supermarket. His dad worked a ton, too, over at the auto body shop. So Cam was used to having the entire house to himself.

He rummaged through the kitchen, searching for a snack and finding a bag of half-eaten nacho chips. He unrolled the bag and plopped down in a living room armchair, near the front window. Then he flipped on the television and mindlessly watched some ridiculous game show as he snacked. His eyes kept flitting over to the window, though, and the moving truck.

As he watched, a woman emerged from the house, followed by a man. The man shouted to

someone inside the back of the moving truck, waving them out.

A boy hopped out of the truck. He had dark, wavy hair, and looked about Cam's age. The boy reached back into the truck, grabbed something, and pulled it down to the driveway.

It was a BMX bike. A Haro, to be exact.

Cam smiled.

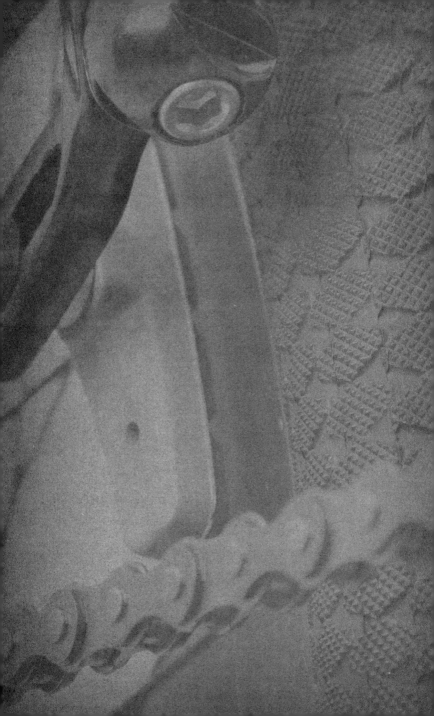

CHAPTER 3

FAST FRIENDS

Cam was still sneaking peeks out the front window when his mom's beat-up station wagon drove past the moving truck and swung into the driveway. A minute later, the side door of the house banged open.

"Little help here, Cameron?" his mom called out. Cam rushed over to see his mom balancing two heavy paper bags with the Kingston Supermarket logo on the side in her arms. Groceries nearly spilled out of both. Cam snagged one of the bags and placed it on the counter.

"Thanks, honey," his mom said. "Did you see we have new neighbors?"

"Yeah," Cam answered. "They have a kid with a Haro BMX bike, too."

"Oh, that's nice. Maybe we should go say hi."

Cam didn't want to seem too anxious, but he was definitely curious to learn more about the new kid. So he helped his mom place the groceries in the cupboards and refrigerator and waited while she changed out of her Kingston uniform. When she returned to the kitchen, she removed some cookies from a jar, set them on a plate, and wrapped it in clear plastic.

The new neighbors were carrying a wooden bed frame toward the house as Cam and his mom walked across the street. Cam looked around for their son, but didn't see him. When the man spied them approaching, he smiled.

"Estella," he said to his wife. "It looks like the welcoming committee has arrived."

He set the bed frame down, and his wife followed suit. He was tall and muscular, with dark, piercing eyes. His wife was a beautiful woman with dark hair pulled into a long ponytail. She swept a stray strand from her face. "Oh," she said. "Hello."

Cam's mom offered her the plate of cookies. "Welcome to the neighborhood." She pointed over her shoulder with her thumb. "We live in the yellow house across the street. I'm Rose Dexter. My husband Thomas is still at work. This is our son, Cameron."

"Cam," he corrected her quietly.

"Hey there, Cam," the man said. He offered his massive hand, and Cam shook it. "I'm Luis Rocca, and this is my wife Estella. So how old are you, Cam? Fourteen?"

"Yes sir."

"A-ha! So is our son, Pedro. He's around here somewhere." Luis glanced around, toward the truck, then the house. He whistled, and seconds

later, the boy Cam had seen earlier poked his head out of the open front door.

"Pedro," Luis said. "Come meet our neighbors."

Pedro jumped down the front steps, shoved his hands into his jeans pockets, and walked across the lawn to join the others.

While the adults spoke, Cam and Pedro stood uncomfortably silent. Finally, Cam said, "I saw you with your bike earlier. Was that a Haro Sport?"

"Yeah," said Pedro. "Best bike ever. You ride?"

"Yeah."

At this, the new kid perked up. "Really? Cool. I hear there's a pretty dope bike park around here."

"Copper Ridge Park," said Cam.

"Nice. So do you race and everything?"

Cam nodded. "You?"

"Little bit. But mainly I just love to ride. BMX, mountain bikes, skateboards. Nothin' better than hitting a jump perfectly, or doing a tail whip and landing on both wheels. Right?"

"Totally." Cam could hardly contain his excitement. Finally, someone who felt the same way about racing that he did.

"So," Pedro said, "we should ride sometime. Maybe we can hit that park?"

"Absolutely."

"Cool."

They chatted for a bit longer, comparing bikes and war stories about biffing. Pedro seemed to have a lot of them, Cam noticed, and a few scars to show for his adventures. Finally, Cam's mom said, "Well, we should let you get back to moving in."

"You mean, get to work eating these delicious-looking cookies," Luis countered. "Am I right?"

Cam's mom smiled and placed her hands on his shoulders. "Come on, hon," she said.

"See ya around," Cam said to Pedro.

"Yeah, man," Pedro said. "See ya."

As Cam and his mom walked back home, Cam thought, *This summer is gonna be epic.*

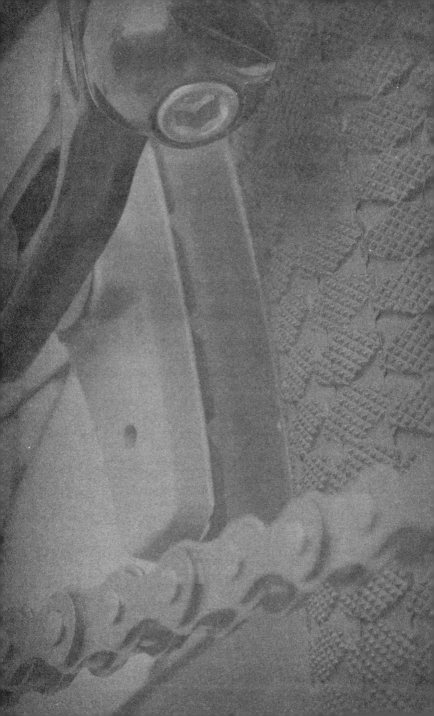

CHAPTER 4

NIGHT RIDERS

Two nights later, and Cam hadn't spoken to Pedro since their first meeting. Cam figured his new neighbor had a lot of stuff to deal with. And it wasn't like Cam was sitting around waiting for Pedro to show up or anything. It was summer, and Cam was spending as much time as he could out at the park riding the practice tracks in anticipation of the competition next month.

The moon was nearly full, casting a blue glow on everything it touched as Cam stepped out of the house and headed over to the detached garage.

He unlocked the deadbolt with the key he wore around his neck and flicked on the light switch located just inside the door. Two bare bulbs dangling from cords in the ceiling sparked to life.

The garage was a sea of bikes. They hung from the rafters and walls, sat propped against the tool bench or flipped upside down with their tires in the air. Cam's dad had been a BMX rider in his youth, and he'd collected a lot of the bikes and gear over the years. A metal rack filled with tools, oil, and boxes of spare parts hung on the far wall. A thin window above the tool bench let in a rectangular hint of moonlight.

This was the spot Cam went when he needed peace and calm. It smelled of chain grease and dust and was pretty close to perfection.

In the middle of the garage was Cam's favorite bike. It'd been a while since he'd checked it over, so he grabbed a set of Allen wrenches and tire tools, pulled up a stool, and sat. Before he went to

work, he slipped in a pair of earbuds and cranked up his music.

Heavy metal pulsed and pounded against his eardrums as he checked the bike's headset and handlebars. He tightened them both before flipping the lightweight bike upside down and inspecting the drivechain.

As he reached over for a red can of chain grease, he thought he heard three loud bangs that weren't in rhythm with the thumping coming from his tunes. He stopped his work and thumbed his music player to silent. His eardrums hummed in the sudden quiet.

Cam sat there, waiting, hearing nothing but the chirp of an insect somewhere inside the garage with him.

Then the sound came again. *Rap! Rap! Rap!*

Cam nearly toppled off his stool. His heart thudded against his chest in fright. He spun around to the window above the tool bench.

Staring back at him was a wide-eyed face.

Cam screamed, stumbling backward.

The figure in the window laughed. "Dude!" a muffled voice said, "It's just me! Pedro!"

Cam relaxed. His speeding heart rate slowed a bit. His shaking hands set down the can of grease. He walked over to the door and opened it.

Pedro slipped inside, like he was a spy being followed and looking for a place to hide. "Hey man," he said. "Sorry to freak you out."

Cam shrugged. "No biggie," he lied.

"Whoa." Pedro spun around on his heel, taking in the garage. "This place is killer." He walked over to the nearest bike, a vintage Hutch, and began to inspect it.

"That was my dad's," Cam said.

"What about those?" Pedro asked. He pointed to a shelf up on the wall. A number of plaques and trophies with small metal bikers popping wheelies on top of them were displayed.

"Oh," Cam said, trying to act nonchalant. "Yeah, those are mine."

Pedro walked over to get a closer look at the trophies. Cam didn't say anything, but he knew exactly what Pedro wouldn't find on the shelves: a trophy that said First Place. There were a lot of third place trophies, even a few second places, too. There were even more of those stupid "participant" trophies and ribbons, the ones everyone gets so they can feel special even though they didn't win.

But Cam had never taken the top prize at any competition.

If Pedro noticed the lack of first place awards, he didn't say anything about it. "Man," he said. "You've been racing for a while."

"Since I was about seven," Cam said. He sat down and went back to cleaning his bike chain.

"You wanna go for a ride?" Pedro asked.

Cam looked up from his work. "Right now? It's pitch-black out there."

"Nah, man. The moon is crazy bright. Besides, I love night biking."

Cam shook his head. "Too dangerous," he said.

"Come on," Pedro pleaded. "I've been cooped up in that house for days now. I wanna see the town."

"I can show you tomorrow," Cam offered.

"My bike's right outside." It was clear that Pedro wasn't letting the issue go easily. "You'll be back before bed time. Live a little, dude."

Cam rolled his eyes. Then he flipped his fully inspected and ready to race BMX back on its wheels. "Fine," he said.

***

Cam loaned one of his helmets to Pedro, and the two boys took off down the street on their bikes. They wove in and out of the pools of yellow light cast by street lamps. And Pedro was right; the moon illuminated their path enough to see where they were going.

Cam was amazed at Pedro's smooth, relaxed riding. He biked through the unfamiliar terrain of Copper Ridge like he'd been doing it his whole life.

They cut down a side street, along the train tracks for a bit. When they hit a hill, and went zipping down, Pedro leaned forward and crouched in his seat. He sailed over the train tracks, executing a barspin and landing it perfectly.

"Dang!" Cam shouted. "Nice move, daredevil!" Then he checked both ways to make sure it was safe, and smartly jumped the tracks to the other side.

They cut through lawns, tearing up grass as they sped along between houses. The inky blackness of the shadows gave Cam pause. He was afraid they'd run into something dangerous. A stray cinderblock. Or a boulder. Or an empty clothesline.

Not Pedro. He moved through it all with a quickness that kept Cam pedaling furiously to

keep up. Around him, crickets chirped and the wind sliced through the trees and made branches whistle.

When the two boys reached the parking lot of Copper Ridge High School, Pedro brought his bike to a screeching halt. "So these are the dreaded halls we'll be navigating in the fall, huh?" he asked.

Cam rode up beside him. "Yeah," he answered. "It's not so bad, though." They dismounted their bikes. Pedro walked to the edge of the lot, and Cam followed. From there, the two boys had a view of the mountains. They were cast in black shadows, like jagged teeth against the star-filled sky.

There were a few spots of twinkling lights in the cliffs. Pedro pointed to one. "What's that?"

"Campsites," Cam answered. "Lot of mountain bike trails up there, too."

"You ever try any of them?"

Cam shook his head. "Not my style. A few of them are pretty dangerous. Like, double black

diamond dangerous. One, the Copper Devil, is supposed to be ridiculous. It's actually closed."

"Really?" Even in the darkness, Cam saw a devious hint of a twinkle in Pedro's eye. For the first time, Cam wondered if there was more to Pedro's racing style than the new kid was sharing.

"Come on," Cam said, walking back and jumping on his bike. "There's a few more stops on our Copper Ridge Night Tour."

They rode through town for another hour, with Cam pointing out town monuments and cool places to go. He showed Pedro the outside of Copper Ridge Dirt Park and went past Benny's Pizzeria, even performing front pogos and manuals through the Kingston Supermarket parking lot.

And though Cam now thought Pedro's style was somewhat reckless, he had to admit: It felt good to have someone riding beside him for once.

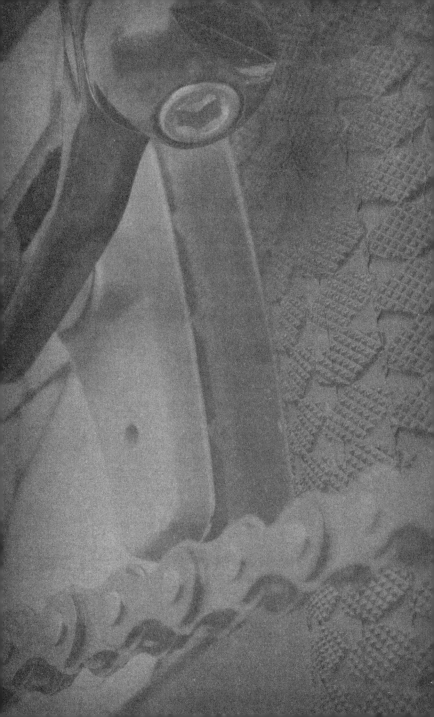

CHAPTER 5

A CRAZY SUGGESTION

Over the next two weeks, Cam and Pedro became inseparable. They were like two sides of a coin, two peas in a pod — all of the crazy metaphors and similes Cam's mom could throw at them. The first time the two boys rode their bikes out to the dirt park, Pedro proclaimed it to be, "The absolute illest place I've ever seen."

When they got there, Cam immediately took his friend to the practice course. "Let's see if you can keep up!" he shouted as he took off down the starting hill. Laughing, Pedro pedaled after him.

They rode side by side for most of the trail. Cam was surprised that Pedro could handle the turns as well as he did, considering how he'd never raced before. He wobbled a bit on the fast-paced berms and nearly biffed. But he recovered nicely in time for a step-down.

When the two boys reached the finish line, Cam could see Pedro was gassed. Still, the noob said, "I wanna . . . try it . . . again."

So they did. Three more times. Then Cam suggested they get a drink of water. As they pedaled past the more difficult Ridge Rider course, Pedro asked, "Why don't we try that one next?"

Cam pretended not to hear his friend, responding with, "There's a cool street course we need to check out. I can teach you how to do a manual or something."

"Wicked," Pedro said.

When they weren't at the course, the two boys were still hanging out. Cam introduced Pedro

to the Benny's "Ultimate Mountain" pizza, a deep-dish pie piled high with meat. "Vegetarians beware!" Pedro shouted in the crowded restaurant as he took his first cheesy bite of pizza goodness.

They also spent a ton of time either working in Cam's garage or hanging out at Pedro's house playing video games on the enormous flat-screen television in the living room. Sports games. Fighting games. Basically any game where they could compete against one another and trash talk while doing it.

It was during one of their epic video game battles — they were facing off in Motocross Mania — when Pedro said, "We should totally take down the Devil."

At first, Cam had no idea what his friend was saying. He thought it had to do with their video game. He continued to jab buttons as his digitized motorbike roared along a street course. "What are you talking about?" he asked.

"The Copper Devil," Pedro answered, matter of fact. "We should ride down the Copper Devil trail."

Cam laughed. But when he looked over at his friend, Pedro's face was stone-serious. He paused the game and turned to face Pedro. "You're kidding, right?"

"No. You've got a couple of bikes we can use, right? BMX-ers ride down mountain trails all the time."

"Maybe professionals do," Cam said. He couldn't believe what Pedro was thinking. "Besides, it's off-limits, man. Closed. Sorry."

"We can do it," Pedro said. "I've seen the way you ride, man. You're good. And life is about taking chances every once in a while, right?"

"If I wanna mix things up, I'll order a different kind of pizza at Benny's," Cam said. "But there's no way I'm riding down Copper Devil."

"Well, I'm going to do it," Pedro said. "Tomorrow morning. With or without you."

Cam didn't know what to say. Riding down the mountain trail would be difficult and dangerous, and it flew in the face of Cam's racing style.

But he wasn't going to let his friend do it alone.

"Fine," he said, caving to the pressure. "I'm in."

Excited, Pedro leaped to his feet. "Yes!" he shouted. "It's gonna be epic!"

Cam wished he believed that.

***

The following day was sunny with a cool breeze cutting across the mountains. It was the perfect day to kick back in a lounge chair with a stack of comic books and an energy drink. That was not, however, what Cam and Pedro had planned.

Cam woke up early, before his parents were out of bed. He'd told them the night before Pedro wanted to check out some of the mountain trails, and his parents had no objections. He kind of just . . . left out . . . the words "Copper" and "Devil," so it wasn't really lying. Because there's no way they'd

let him near the treacherous trail without an adult with them.

In the garage, Cam picked out a pair of mountain bikes. They were larger than BMX bikes with more durable frames and wider tires. He checked the two bikes out and found them in great shape. He filled his backpack with snacks and a large Nalgene water bottle. After double-checking everything, he wheeled the bikes over to Pedro's house.

Mrs. Rocca was out in the front yard, kneeling in a flower garden and weeding plants. "Hello, Cameron," she said as he approached. "What a beautiful day."

"Hi, Mrs. Rocca." Cam felt immediately guilty. He was afraid, for some reason, that he'd spill the beans about his and Pedro's plan.

Thankfully, he didn't have to say much else, because Pedro came bursting out the front door. He shouldered his backpack. "See ya later, Mom,"

he said as he ran over to Cam. He pointed eagerly at the bikes. "Which one is mine?"

Cam pushed one over to him.

"Sweet." Pedro caught the bike and leaped onto it.

"You boys have fun," Mrs. Rocca said, waving one of her dirty, gloved hands. "And stay safe."

"We will!" Pedro shouted as he began to pedal off down the road.

Cam followed, trying to shake Mrs. Rocca's parting words from his head. And failing.

The ride up the side of the mountain, to the site where the Copper Devil started, took them nearly an hour. It wasn't a particularly steep route. It wove back and forth, gradually inclining. Still, the going was tough, and the boys stopped a few times at scenic overlooks just off the road. "At least we won't have to pedal this hard on the way down," Pedro joked.

Cam didn't laugh.

Finally, they reached the last rise. Beyond, Cam saw the campgrounds and the start of many hiking and biking trails. There was a small ranger cabin as well, tucked in a stand of tall trees. Cam didn't see anyone inside. Next to the cabin was a large map with various trails highlighted and a sign with a list of warnings. Things like: *Never bike alone. Always have a phone with you. Stay hydrated.*

Pedro wheeled over to the map, studied it, and found Copper Devil. He looked around the area a bit. "There," he said, pointing to a section of flat stone to their right. A sign and a pair of bright orange wooden barricades blocked the trail entrance.

Cam tried one final time to talk some sense into his friend. "Are you sure you want to do this?"

"One hundred percent," Pedro said, casually riding over to the beginning of the trail. Cam followed. He gripped his handlebars tight, glanced around to see if anyone was watching.

Maybe it won't be so bad, he thought. Maybe Pedro's right. You're a talented rider. You've got this.

Pedro looked back at Cam. He wiggled his eyebrows and tightened his helmet strap. "And away we go," he said, weaving between the barricades and pushing off down the Copper Devil with Cam not far behind.

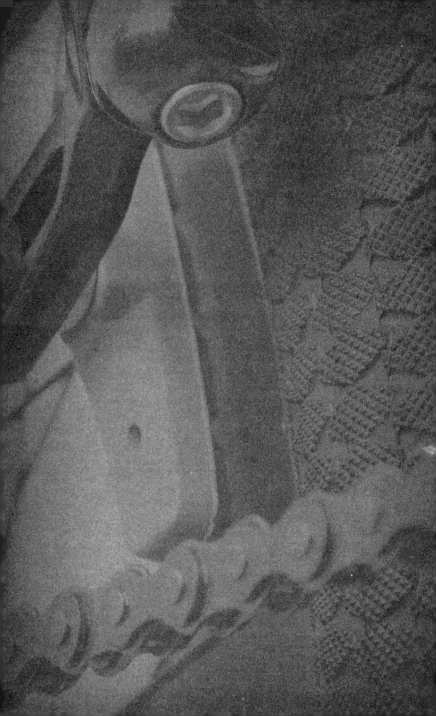

CHAPTER 6

RIDING DOWN THE DEVIL

Cam slowly descended the rocky trail. Large boulders reached for the sky on either side of him. Other riders who'd braved the Devil had carved a path of hard-packed earth between the rocks. Ahead, Pedro was standing on his pedals, weaving back and forth.

It's actually not that bad, Cam thought, which he immediately regretted because that pretty much guaranteed that something terrible would happen.

But the first half-mile or so of the trail was relatively easy. They passed through a section of

tall, dried weeds that waved in the breezy morning air. Pedro reached out and swiped at them with one gloved hand.

"This is a Sunday stroll, man," he said over his shoulder to Cam.

Right before the trail made a markedly steep drop, the two boys stopped. Pausing for rest on a plateau of rock, they chugged water from their bottles, and Cam noshed on a granola bar.

Pedro looked around. "It's beautiful up here," he said. "And so quiet."

Cam secured his water bottle back onto his bike, and the two continued down the trail. Cam's shocks worked overtime as he bounced and jounced over rocks and loose stones. He tried to maintain some sort of control and an even speed, but it became pointless. Pedro didn't seem to have the same fear, and his lead on Cam grew considerably. Once, he even turned back to holler, "Hurry up, Grandma!"

Back and forth, they wove down the mountain. Trees whooshed by on either side, then sharp rocks. Ahead, Cam could see what looked like a ravine cut into the earth, and a makeshift jump. Pedro lowered his head, barreling down the mountainside. The ground was looser here, likely the result of a recent flash-flood. It was much harder to maneuver.

"Pedro!" Cam shouted. "Be careful!"

But the fearless teen either didn't hear him or couldn't stop his momentum. He hit the jump at top speed, and was about to soar into the air, when his back wheel skidded through a large patch of loose stones. Pedro's bike spun out, sending him over the handlebars.

Pedro cursed loudly as he fell. His arms flailed as he tumbled down into the ravine, rolling down through grass and dirt until he was out of sight.

"Pedro!" Cam rushed down to help his friend. Not too fast, though. He didn't want to suffer the

same fate. As he approached the lip of the jump, he brought his bike to a screeching halt.

Cam dismounted and looked down into the ravine. Lying on a small hillside about ten feet below was Pedro. His bike was nearby, its front wheel twisted and bent, its handlebars cracked.

Pedro was clutching his left leg at the thigh. A grimace of pain contorted his face.

Cam climbed down to his friend and knelt beside him.

"I think it's . . . broken," Pedro said.

Cam's stomach turned to stone, and a sense of dread washed over him.

Pedro nodded, tried to pull himself up. "Yeah, it's . . . *ow*!" He cursed and laid back down.

"I don't know what to do," Cam admitted. He peeled off his helmet and backpack and dropped them in the dirt.

"Call for help." Pedro spoke through gritted teeth. His face, twisted in pain, was smeared with

dirt. A thin trickle of blood ran from a cut on his forehead and down over his left eyebrow.

"Good idea." Cam unzipped his bag and rummaged around for his phone. He found it, thumbed it on, and got a 'Searching' symbol. "No service," he said. He tried to keep the panic out of his voice.

"'Kay," Pedro said. He was quieter now. "Gimme a couple of minutes. Maybe then . . . I can try to . . . stand again."

The two minutes they sat side by side in the dirt felt like an eternity. Cam tried to get his heart to stop racing but couldn't. He slid his hands under his legs to hide how badly they were shaking.

Finally, Pedro reached out. "Help me . . . up," he croaked. His breathing was ragged now.

Cam crouched, sliding Pedro's arm over his shoulder. With all his might, he attempted to lift his friend upright again.

Pedro let out a fresh cry of pain.

"Sorry! Sorry!" Cam set him back down.

Pedro shook his head. "It's no use," he said. "I'm not going anywhere. You'll have to . . . go for help."

"Go for help?" said Cam. "By myself?"

Pedro's face gave Cam the answer.

Cam knew what his friend was suggesting, but he didn't want to believe it. It was one thing to tackle the dangerous trail with another person. But to do it alone?

If I fall — if something happens to me like it happened to Pedro — we're both going to be in serious trouble.

But he couldn't think of another way. Pedro definitely needed help, and he needed it quickly. Cam knew there was another ranger station at the bottom of the mountain. He knew that an emergency crew could easily reach Pedro and get him to safety.

What Cam didn't know — what actually frightened him — was whether or not he could muster the courage to ride the Copper Devil solo.

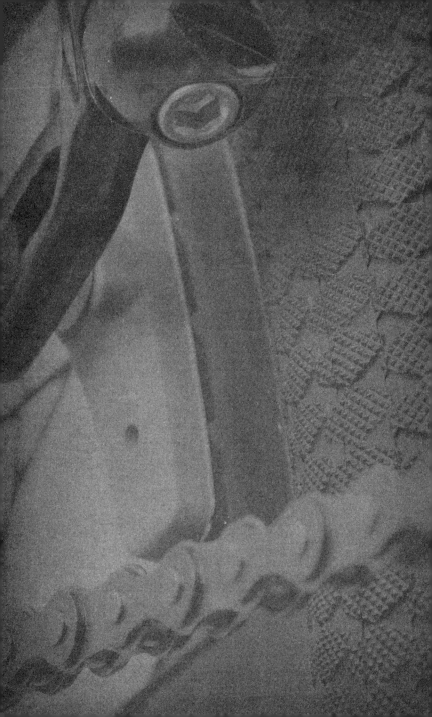

CHAPTER 7

FACING FEAR

"Suck it up, Cam," he said to himself, standing at the lip of the jump, staring at the trail as it wove down the mountain and was swallowed by rocks. "You can do this."

Cam was Pedro's only hope. So he took one long, steadying breath, tried to calm his frayed nerves, and made the only logical decision he could.

He retrieved his bike from the jump and carefully wheeled it down into the ravine. When he reached Pedro, he set it down momentarily as he

dug another energy bar out of his pack, unstrapped his water bottle from the bike's frame, and placed both it and his bag next to Pedro.

"You'll need the supplies more than I will," he said. "Water, too."

Pedro didn't have the strength to argue. He nodded weakly.

Cam placed a hand firmly on his friend's shoulder and tucked his cell phone into Pedro's palm. "Keep trying for a signal. Help will be here soon. Okay?"

"Roger that," Pedro said.

Cam raised a fist. Pedro smiled thinly and bumped it.

Cam walked his bike to the far side of the ravine, and up the slight incline to the other side. There, the trail picked up again. He straddled the bike, strapped on his helmet, and twisted the handlebars nervously.

"Now or never," he whispered.

Cam took one last look at his friend, pushed off, and began to descend the mountain again.

He immediately felt how steep the trail had become. Despite his best efforts, he found himself moving faster than before. Over a smooth boulder. Bunny-hopping down to the stone floor. Carving around a patch of trees. Over a set of man-made berms.

The path split, separated, and disappeared altogether. Cam alertly followed a groove in the path where other riders had created their own trail. His eyes darted left and right. He squeezed the brakes — but not too hard — to keep from spilling. There was no time to think about his moves. He simply rode one mile, then another. Down a steep hill. Right toward the mountain.

Ahead, a thin, vertical opening was cut in the side of the stone. It loomed ahead like the earth had split in two. Cam barreled toward it. He didn't dare brake for fear that he'd swerve and crash.

He sailed into the narrow opening, the two cliffs barely a foot away from each of his shoulders. Cam held his breath as he threaded downhill. At the bottom, he saw what looked like another ravine, another jump.

A huge jump.

He squeezed the brakes out of instinct. His back wheel kicked out, struck one side of the cliff. "Oh no!" he shouted, his voice bouncing off the rocks. He released the brake, wrestling with the handlebars, hoping to regain control.

And did.

But there was no time to breathe relief. The jump was approaching. It was enormous, wider than even the triple at the end of Ridge Rider.

There was no time to be afraid.

Cam pedaled hard, leaned low, and hit the jump at full speed.

He rocketed into the air.

It felt like he hung in the sky for a lifetime.

That he was never coming down. He glanced to the rocks below, saw where he was supposed to land, and tapped his brake. Then he angled his front wheel toward the patch of earth below, and hit it perfectly.

His shocks absorbed the impact.

"Yes!" Cam shouted.

The rest of the trail was a series of cutbacks and berms. He rode through a copse of trees, tall ash and spruce and white poplars. Soon, he saw the ranger cabin at the base of the hill, a red Jeep parked beside it.

Cam was spent. He wanted lie in the dirt and catch his breath. But Pedro was counting on him. He mustered up the last bits of strength he had and maneuvered down the hill. He came to a stuttering stop near the cabin.

Cam dismounted, staggered to the cabin door, and knocked.

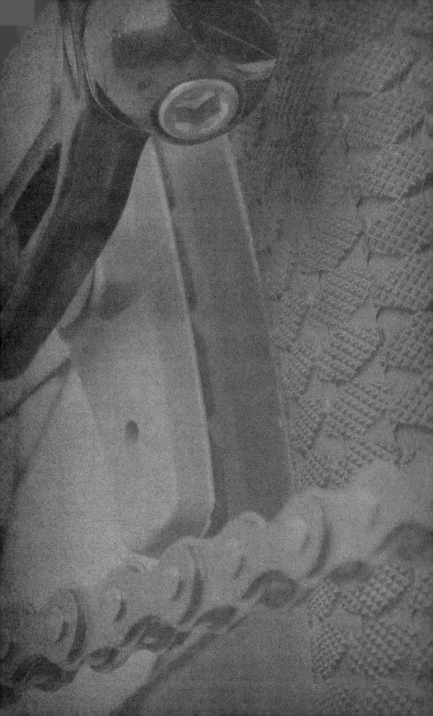

CHAPTER 8

GROUNDED

The park ranger, a man in his twenties wearing a tan uniform and hat, sat behind a desk. He leapt to his feet when Cam rushed through the door.

"Is everything all right?" the ranger asked.

Cam shook his head. "My friend . . . " he stammered. "Up . . . on the trail."

"Trail? Which trail?"

"Copper Devil."

The ranger's face turned ashen. He didn't doubt that Cam was telling the truth. And so he picked up the phone on his desk and immediately called the paramedics.

After he'd spoken with them, he held the phone out to Cam. "You best call your parents, young man," he said. "I'll send someone up the trail to be with your friend."

Cam hesitated before taking the phone. He knew what his parents would say, and a very large part of him would rather race down Copper Devil again than face his father.

Soon, while waiting outside the ranger's cabin, the steady rhythm of helicopter rotors approached, and a red emergency chopper roared overhead. Cam shoved his hands in his pockets, hoping to keep them from shaking.

This is crazy scary, he thought.

Cam's parents and the Roccas rode together out to the park. Cam had been right. The look he received from his father as he exited the car made it pretty easy for Cam to guess how much trouble he was in for lying.

I'm gonna be grounded for life.

A small camera crew stood nearby, as well. They were from the local television station. When they'd approached Cam and his parents for comments, his dad had brushed them off and said, "Take your slow news day elsewhere."

A short time later, the red chopper crested the mountain again, vibrant against the blue sky. One of the paramedics, walkie-talkie in hand, approached Pedro's parents. "They're taking him straight to Copper Ridge Hospital," she explained, shouting to be heard over the helicopter noise. "He has a broken tibia."

Pedro's mom clasped a hand over her mouth, trying to stifle a horrified gasp. The sound that escaped into the air felt like a tiny dagger in Cam's heart.

Soon the helicopter disappeared over the tree line. Cam followed his parents back to their car, climbing in the back with Pedro's parents. The boys' bikes were strapped to the rack on top.

The ride to the hospital was silent and uncomfortable. Cam couldn't even look at the adults. He stared out the side window, rested his head against the glass.

"It was Pedro's idea, wasn't it?" Estella's voice was timid as she spoke to Cam. Luis had his arm around her shoulder. Her eyes were red from crying. "Riding down the dangerous trail," she said. "It was Pedro's idea?"

"We both knew how risky it was," Cam said quietly. He saw his dad's piercing eyes in the rearview mirror and said nothing more.

When they reached the hospital emergency room, they were told that Pedro was in surgery, and that the doctors would let everyone know when it was okay to see him.

Cam's mom hugged Estella. "Please keep us updated on how he's doing," she said, turning to Cam. "Come on, Cameron. Let's go."

"Can't I wait 'til he's out of surgery?" Cam said.

"You'll see him soon." She slid an arm over Cam's shoulders.

"I'll let him know you're worried," Luis said to Cam. Then he added, "Thank you for your bravery today."

Cam nodded, but said nothing. He didn't feel very brave at all.

***

The tension on the car ride home hung thick in the air. Cam knew his dad was a ticking time bomb, and that any minute now, he'd unleash the pent-up emotions he'd been holding in.

Finally, as they passed Benny's and went under the banner for the upcoming competition, his dad said, "I don't care whose idea it was to ride down that trail. You're kids, not professional bikers."

"But Dad — "

"It's closed for a reason, Cameron," his dad continued. "You know better."

"Yes, sir."

"You're grounded for a month. No phone, no dirt track. Got it?"

"But the competition!" Cam said. "The BMX races are in less than a month!"

His dad turned into their driveway. "I'm well aware of that."

"So I can't compete?"

"I haven't decided yet."

"That's so unfair!"

"I'm not sure you've earned it."

When the car finally swung into the driveway and came to a stop, Cam banged open his door and ran to the garage before his parents could protest. He used the key around his neck to open it, and slammed it hard behind him.

Anger coursed through his veins, and hot tears flooded his eyes and ran down his cheeks. He pawed them away with one hand. Sure, he'd caved to peer pressure, had followed Pedro down the trail instead of trying harder to talk his friend out

of going. But he'd also done something on a BMX than he'd never done before. And it felt like all of that had been stripped away.

Cam kicked over a nearby bike, one of his dad's Haro Sports. Then he pushed over the array of tools lined up on the tool bench. They clattered and rattled on the garage's cement floor. Finally, he snatched one of the trophies off his shelf — his fourth place prize from last summer's BMX Grand Prix in Salt Lake City — and flung it at the wide metal garage door. It shattered into small pieces on the floor. Cam's heart felt the same way as the trophy looked.

***

Pedro was not shy about telling people how he got his bright blue leg cast. There was a report on the news, and they'd interviewed him while he was still in the hospital. The teen had smiled for the camera and said, "My buddy Cam biked down the Copper Devil to get help."

Cam saw his injured friend every once in a while when his parents said it was okay. The two boys mostly hung out in lawn chairs in Pedro's front yard or worked in Cam's garage. Pedro had to hobble around on a pair of crutches.

One morning, as the two boys hung out in the garage while Cam worked on Pedro's bent handlebars, Pedro said, "BMX competition is in a few days. Your dad gonna let you compete?"

Cam shrugged. "Dunno. We haven't really talked about it, so . . . probably not."

"That sucks."

"Yep."

"Totally unfair."

"That's what I told him."

"I'll see what I can do."

Cam laughed, but when he looked up at Pedro, he saw that his friend was not smiling. And that twinkle had returned to his eye.

That night, long after Pedro had gone home

for dinner, Cam flicked off the lights in the garage and locked up. He walked into the house to find his friend seated at the dining room table opposite his dad. The sight took him aback. "What are you doing here, dude?" he asked.

Pedro said nothing.

Cam's dad had both muscular arms resting on the table. His baseball cap, thick with grease from work, sat perched on his head.

He motioned to an empty chair. "Sit," he said.

Cam did.

His dad exhaled, chewed on his bottom lip for a moment, and then said, "Pedro has brought it to my attention—again—that he was the one responsible for your little . . . trip down the Copper Devil."

"Heh. Trip," Pedro said with a chuckle. He rapped his knuckles on his blue cast. "That's one word for it."

"What you did, Cam, was reckless and

dangerous and against everything I've taught you about bike safety," his dad continued. "But I also know how much this competition means to you."

Cam felt a flicker of hope bloom in his chest. No way, he thought. This can't be happening.

"Now, I don't know if I'm doing this because you deserve it, or because Pedro's finally worn me down — "

"It's probably both," Pedro chimed in.

" — but you're still signed up out at the dirt park. So I'm going to allow you the opportunity to compete."

Cam leaped out of his chair so quickly that it toppled to the floor. "Yes!" he shouted. "Thank you, thank you, thank you!" He bumped fists with Pedro. Then he went over and hugged his dad.

"All right," his dad said with a smile. "You've only got a couple of days to practice and to make sure your bike is in peak condition," he said. "You better get to work."

Cam helped Pedro to his feet, and the two boys excitedly ran — hobbled, in Pedro's case — back out to the garage together.

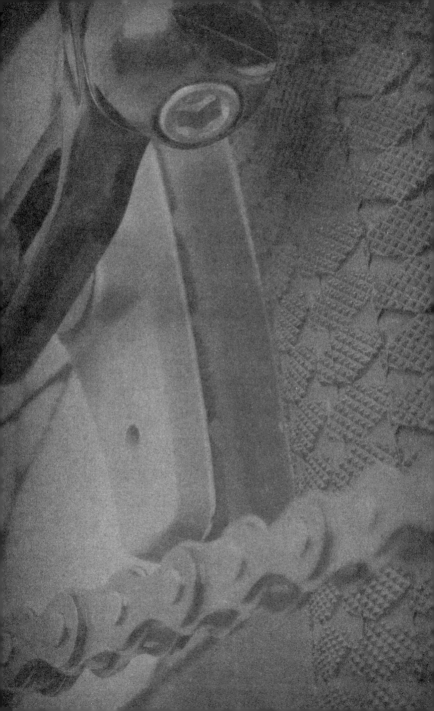

CHAPTER 9

A DAY AT THE RACES

Cam had been to plenty of races before, so he knew what to expect. But he'd never been to one at his home track, and had never seen Copper Ridge Dirt Park so jam-packed with people before. The parking lot overflowed with cars and news vans whose antenna poles rose from their roofs and into the sky.

Pedro leaned on one of his crutches, taking in the whole thing.

"Let's go sign in," Cam said, pulling his bike out of the back of his parents' station wagon.

While his parents parked the car, Cam and Pedro entered the dirt park. Kids of all ages were swarming about. Many rode the practice courses. Others tried to distract themselves from the competition by performing 360s and boomerangs on the nearby street course and vert ramp. Tables and tents filled with merchandise and sponsors lined the park's fences. People shoved free samples and gift bags at Pedro, who eagerly accepted them.

Cam found the sign-in tent, and a young guy with a shaved head covered in tattoos looked him up and gave him a number—four ninety-three—to pin onto his chest. "You're in moto seven of eight for your age group," he explained. "Should be up in about an hour."

The man looked over at Pedro.

"I'm his coach," Pedro joked.

The man shook his head and smiled, then tossed Pedro a badge on a lanyard.

They walked out of the tent.

Pedro asked, "What the heck is a moto?"

"It's just the BMX way of saying what group I'm in," Cam said. "In this type of competition, the winner of each moto races in the finals."

"Gotcha."

They found a spot near the Ridge Rider track to watch the other motos. Just seeing the supercross track made Cam anxious. But then he thought about the Copper Devil and how he'd managed to race down it when he didn't let his head get in the way of his bike. His nerves seemed to calm a bit.

Cam's parents soon joined them. As they were old pros at spectating, Cam didn't worry about them. A combination of surprise and excitement coursed through Cam as he spied Jack, Ayla, and Peter—the three kids he raced against the day Pedro moved to Copper Ridge. Jack raced in moto two. Cam cheered him on.

"Do you know him?" Pedro asked. "He looks pretty good."

Cam nodded. "He's a great racer. Tough to beat."

Pedro pointed his crutch at the track just as Jack crossed the finish line, well ahead of the others. "Looks like it."

Ayla was in moto four. The determined racer started out soundly. She positioned herself well in the first turn and never looked back, soaring past the finish line in first place. She skidded to a stop near Jack, and the two bumped fists.

Peter, unfortunately, didn't fare as well. He had trouble on one of the turns, cutting a corner too close and scraping against a fellow racer. The two struggled to maintain their balance, but both wound up tumbling to the dirt. The spill looked rough, but both riders quickly got to their feet and gave the officials a thumbs-up to let them know they were all right.

Finally, the man operating the park's sound system said in a deep voice, "Riders for moto

seven, please report to the track. Moto seven, report to track."

"That's me," Cam said.

"Good luck," his mom said.

"Have a clean race," his dad said, his face set like it always was at a competition, a mixture of pride and worry.

"Break a leg!" Pedro said. Then he added, "Oh, wait . . . . "

Cam laughed. His friend had found a way to relieve a bit of tension, even if it was only temporary. He walked his bike over to Ridge Rider's start ramp. Several of the other racers were already there. They all said "Hey" to one another. One of the kids even nodded at Cam and said, "Aren't you the kid who rode Copper Devil?"

"Yeah," Cam answered.

"Sick, man. I saw that on the news."

They lined up in their spots near the gate. Cam was near the inside of the track, a good place to hit

the first turn. He slid his goggles into place, made sure his helmet was tight.

Cam took a deep breath. *I hope I did enough to prepare*, he thought. Any time away from the track could easily affect his chances. Couple that with the fact that he'd actually never won a competition before?

Cam shook his head and slapped the side of his helmet to clear his thoughts.

Concentrate. Focus.

"Racers, on your mark!" shouted an official at the side of the track.

Cam gripped his handlebars, leaned forward. His foot twitched anxiously on his pedal.

Then the gate dropped and they were off!

The mass of racers flew down the ramp and onto the track. Dirt and dust plumed up in their wake. It was an utter frenzy. They hit the first turn quick, and Cam leaned his bike low and swung through it with ease. He could feel the rust and

discomfort flaking away, and shrugged it off. After the turn, he — along with four others — were in the front of the pack.

Next were the small berms. He navigated them well, letting his bike handle the shock and moving in stride with the small mounds of earth. They reminded him of the bumpy terrain on the Copper Devil.

By the time they made it through the second turn, Cam was pulling ahead. Only two other racers kept pace with him.

"Come on, Cam!" he heard Pedro shout from the crowd. The words of encouragement pushed him to pedal harder over the first large jump. He caught air, tapped his brake, and came down perfectly. One of the other racers did not, and she wiped out in the dirt. The crowd gasped.

Cam and the remaining racer hit the last turn. Cam was ahead, but he didn't dare look over his shoulder to see exactly how far.

The triple jump loomed like a curse ahead of him. He gathered as much speed as he could, pedaled hard up the first jump, and launched himself into the air.

He didn't have enough speed. He knew it. It was happening all over again. Cam was going to bail, and lose, and wind up with just another participant ribbon for his wall. As he came back down, the only thing he could do was squeeze his brake, land on the backside of the second jump, and hope he had enough left in the tank to pedal up the final hill.

Adrenaline coursed through his veins. He landed, swooped down the second jump, and pedaled up the third. Behind him, he heard the other racer catch major air.

It's gonna be close.

Cam hit the last jump. He saw the other racer out of the corner of his eye. They both came down at the same time, tires crunching and churning in

the dirt. Together, they blasted past the finish line.

Cam brought his bike to a stop. He swung his head left and right, searching for the leader board.

Did I win? he thought.

Cam, the other racer, and the entire crowd, held their collective breaths and waited for the board to flash the winner.

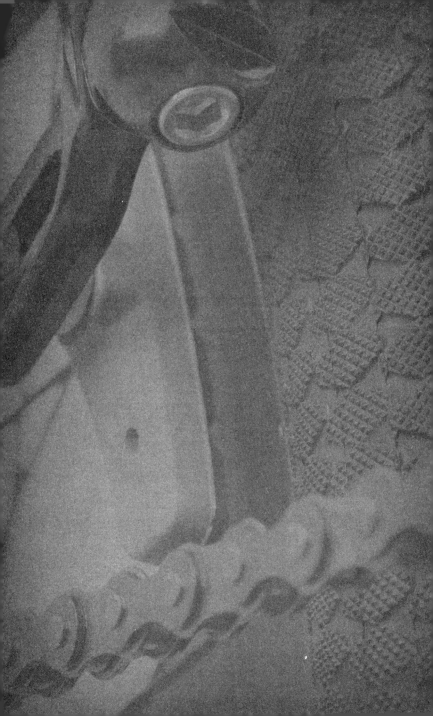

CHAPTER 10

FULL SPEED AHEAD

Seconds stretched to minutes . . . to, seemingly, hours, to eons. The leader board stayed blank. No winner was announced. The entire dirt park was silent with anticipation.

Finally, a voice boomed over the loudspeaker. *The winner of moto seven is racer number nine-four-three. Cameron Dexter.*

He'd done it. Even though he'd messed up the stupid triple jump—again—he'd won his qualifying race by the skin of his teeth. Cam draped himself over his handlebars, exhausted and elated.

His parents and Pedro fought their way through the crowd to be at his side. "That was insane!" Pedro shouted, grabbing Cam by the shoulders and shaking him.

"Great race, Cam," his dad said, while his mom offered him a quick squeeze.

Cam laughed. "Thanks. But I haven't won anything yet. The real test is still to come."

After the last batch of racers finished their qualifying run, the booming voice on the loudspeaker said, "Championship race for ages fourteen to sixteen in five minutes. Five minutes."

While the other racers prepared, Cam sat with his eyes closed. He pictured the triple jump over and over, wondering how he could get enough speed out of the turn, wondering if he'd ever be able to hit it just right.

"You're overthinking it." Pedro was standing behind him, leaning against his crutch again.

"I don't think I can make it, man," Cam said.

"Yeah, and you didn't think you could ride down Copper Devil. But — oh wait! — you did. And you rocked it. Be brave, dude."

The weight on Cam's shoulders seemed to lift, however briefly. "Thanks," he said.

"Hey man. It's what I'm here for." He held up his tote bag filled with free merchandise. "Well, that and free swag."

With a final word of encouragement, Cam made his way to the ramp. He lined up with the others, getting his first chance to see Jack and Ayla. Jack recognized him and nodded. Ayla lined up next to him. "Good luck," she said.

"Back at ya," said Cam.

They bumped fists.

"Racers to your mark!" the nearby official shouted. Cam did a final check of his bike and his equipment.

"You got this, Cam!" Pedro hollered from the sea of spectators.

Clang! The gate dropped.

Cam shot down the ramp at breakneck speed. Elbows bumped and nudged and wheels came millimeters away from colliding as he and the other racers zipped toward the first turn.

He hit the turn, effortlessly carving his way through. Unlike the last race, all of the competitors made it. They rode en masse over the series of berms, looking like a sea of turbulent waves. Cam was near the front of the pack, and as they reached the second turn, he rode low, trying to gain ground. Jack was there, right beside him. They came out of the turn together, with Jack half of a bike's length ahead.

Like always, Cam was in second place.

They held strong this way until the last turn. As Cam came around it, he started to squeeze his brake. He anticipated the approaching triple jump. But he knew that if he slowed down now, he'd never have enough speed to make it over.

Cam let up on the brake, leaned forward, and pedaled hard. His legs chugged like the pistons of a massive steam engine.

The jump vanished in his mind. The racers were dust, the course was a mountain trail. He was back on the Copper Devil, riding through the crack in the mountain, about to hit the ravine jump.

He dug hard, felt his heart thundering in his chest.

This is it.

Cam blasted off the triple jump like he'd been shot out of a cannon. The crowd roared its approval as he cut through the air so high, he felt like he could touch the clouds. He thought to prep for his landing, to tilt his wheel down.

Not this time, he thought.

He needed every millisecond.

Cam's bike wheels hit the dirt. The frame shuddered and wobbled. In a blur of motion, he crossed the finish line with no one ahead of him.

He'd done it.

He'd won!

The feeling of victory was more overwhelming than he could have ever imagined. The other racers zipped past him as they all finished the race. Cam ripped his helmet and goggles off. He took a breath and pumped a fist in the air. He saw Pedro waving his crutch over the crowd. His mom and dad, standing beside his excited friend, beamed with pride.

As he regained his breath, other racers came over to congratulate him, Ayla and Jack included. It was all a blur that didn't feel real until the announcer called his name later that afternoon, and he stepped onto a stage to receive his trophy.

"Congratulations," the official said as he handed over a gleaming, golden trophy. It was heavy and wonderful and Cam couldn't believe it was all his. He pointed to the crowd, to Pedro specifically, and gave him a thumbs-up. If it wasn't

for his new friend, Cam wouldn't be standing up on stage at all.

He kissed the trophy, then held it aloft. The crowd cheered on all sides of him.

It was the most amazing feeling in the world.

ABOUT THE AUTHOR

Brandon Terrell is the author of numerous children's books, including several volumes in both the *Tony Hawk 900 Revolutions* series and the *Tony Hawk Live 2 Skate* series. He has also written the first four titles from the *Sports Illustrated Kids Time Machine Magazine* set, due for publication in 2016. When not hunched over his laptop, Brandon enjoys watching movies and television, reading, watching (and playing!) baseball, and spending time with his wife and two children in Minnesota.

GLOSSARY

bail (BAYL)—to jump off in order to avoid a crash

berm (BURM)—a mound or wall of earth

black diamond (BLAK DIE-mund)—a difficult trail or ski slope

daredevil (DAYR-dev-uhl)—a person who does dangerous things, especially for attention

drive chain (DRIYV CHAYN)—an endless chain with links that meet up with toothed wheels in order to transmit power

epic (EH-pik)—particularly impressive, remarkable, or excellent

maneuver (muh-NOO-vuhr)—a careful or skillful action or movement

moto (MOH-toh)—any of the heats in a moto-cross or BMX contest

supercross (SOO-puhr CROS)—a motorcycle race held on a dirt track having hairpin turns and high jumps

vintage (VIN-tuhj)—dating from the past

DISCUSSION QUESTIONS

1. Why do you think that Cam is so cautious in the beginning of the story? Talk about the advantages and disadvantages of being cautious when engaged in sporting competition.

2. When Pedro moved into Cam's neighborhood, he influenced Cam's riding style. Has a friend, family member, or classmate ever influenced you to make changes in the way you do things?

3. When Pedro injures himself riding down the Copper Devil, Cam makes a split decision to ride down the rest of the Copper Devil to get help. What would have happened if Cam was also injured? Discuss your answer. Talk about a time when you had to make a quick decision.

WRITING PROMPTS

1. Cam and Pedro are really into BMXing. Think about your own hobbies and choose one of them to write a one-page essay about. Why do you enjoy this particular hobby? Was there someone that inspired your interest? Be sure to describe all pertinent details.

2. When Cam and Pedro ride down the Copper Devil and Pedro is injured, Cam knows that he'll be in trouble with his parents. Write about a time that you disappointed someone.

3. When Pedro moved into Cam's neighborhood, the two became fast friends. Write a short "friends" picture book story for younger readers. Let the kid in you come out by making sure to illustrate with colorful pictures!

BMX FACTS!

BMX is short for Bicycle Moto Cross.

BMX was invented in the late 1960s in Southern California. It was created because of the popularity of motocross, or off-road motorcycle racing.

A standard BMX bike is smaller than an average road bike and has a fixed frame. It also only has one gear, which makes racing easier. There are three specific bike models: traditional, freestyle, and jump.

An average BMX race lasts about 25 to 40 seconds, and racers reach speeds up to 35 miles (56 kilometers) per hour!

Dirt racetracks usually measure about 1,000 feet (305 meters)in length.

BMX is also an Olympic sport. It became a medal sport in the 2008 Summer Games in Beijing, China.

KILLER MOVES!

BUNNY-HOP — A bunny-hop is when both the front and back wheel of your BMX jump off the ground at the same time. It's used to jump over small obstacles.

TAIL WHIP — To perform a tail whip, catch air and rotate your BMX frame once around the bars, which remain stationary.

X-UP — After going off a jump, spin your BMX's handlebars 180 degrees, so that your arms form the letter X. Quickly rotate them back before landing. This is an X-Up!

BARSPIN — To complete a barspin, hop your BMX into the air. Throw your handlebars so they spin while you're mid-jump, and catch them before you land.

FRONT POGO — A 'pogo' can be done on either your front or back wheel. For a front pogo, apply your front and rear brakes until the back wheel comes off the ground. Then hop on the front wheel like you would on a pogo stick!

MANUAL — A manual is basically riding your BMX on the back wheel, with the front wheel up in the air for a long period of time. Use your arms and legs to maintain your balance.